Ms Dhaliwal

*McGraw-Hill*
*Children's Publishing*

*A Division of The McGraw·Hill Companies*

This edition published in the United States of America in 2003
by McGraw-Hill Children's Publishing, a division of The McGraw-Hill Companies.

Send all inquiries to:
McGraw-Hill Children's Publishing
8787 Orion Place
Columbus, OH 43240-4027

www.MHkids.com

Printed in China.

1-56189-308-0

Library of Congress Cataloging-in-Publication Data on file with the publisher.

1 2 3 4 5 6 7 8 9 BRI 07 06 05 04 03 02

First published in Great Britain in 2002 by Brimax
An imprint of Octopus Publishing Group Ltd
2-4 Heron Quays, London E14 4JP

# Little Star

Written and illustrated by

## Arcadio Lobato

Mc Graw Hill **McGraw-Hill**
**Children's Publishing**

One clear summer night in a sleepy little village, frogs croaked and crickets chirped.

Little Star didn't understand that it was just a bedtime story. He dreamed of meeting the princess, visiting the palace, and seeing the herd of elephants. He wanted to be the star that the princess plucked from the night sky.

Little Star slipped away from the larger stars who watched over him. Following the echo of Helen's mother's words, he floated gently to Earth.

While a little girl named Helen got ready for bed, warm lights glowed in open windows of her house and hundreds of stars sparkled brightly in the night sky.

After Helen snuggled under the covers, her mother read her a fairy tale as she did every night.

"Once upon a time, there was a beautiful princess," her mother began. As she read, the words floated up over the trees and through the night sky to the clouds.

High above, shining with a soft, blue light, Little Star listened.

This night's story was about a princess who lived in a golden palace. She had riches beyond imagination, the finest clothes in all the land, and even a herd of elephants. But the princess's greatest wish was to pick a star from the sky and keep it for her very own.

Little Star listened to the tale in wonder. By the end of the story, Helen had fallen sound asleep.

Helen woke up to a soft, blue light shining in her eyes. She was surprised to see a tiny star, just outside her bedroom window.

"I must be dreaming," said Helen.

"Hello, Princess," said Little Star. He twinkled as he spoke. "I have found you at last! I am the star you wished for. Will you show me your palace, your fine clothes, and your herd of elephants?"

Helen frowned. "I'm not a princess. I'm just an ordinary little girl in an ordinary house. My name is Helen."

"You aren't a princess?" Little Star began to cry blue, sparkly tears.

Helen felt sorry for the star. "I know!" she said. "I'll be Princess Helen just for tonight and show you my kingdom. Come with me."

Helen wrapped her blanket around her shoulders. It floated
behind her like a velvety cloak. To Little Star, she had become
the beautiful princess from the story.

Helen then greeted the croaking frogs, the singing crickets,
the glowworms, and a neighbor's cat as if she owned all the land.
"These are my loyal subjects," Helen told Little Star.

"And this is my golden palace." Helen pointed to her house. Lights glowed from the windows, and flowers decorated the window boxes.

"It's beautiful," whispered Little Star.

Since there were no elephants in Helen's neighborhood, she led Little Star to the goats and pigs that lived nearby. "These are the animals that live in my kingdom," explained Helen.

Little Star blinked happily. "I've never seen anything like them," he said.

Suddenly, a bright red light floated down from the night sky. It was a large star, and it did not look pleased. Helen took a step back and clutched her blanket.

"What are you doing down here, Little Star?" The red star pulsed slowly and sternly. "You know that stars cannot leave the sky. It's time to come back home now!"

"But why?" cried Little Star. "I am having so much fun here with Princess Helen. I am the star she wished for, and I want to stay."

"I'm afraid that is not possible," explained the older and wiser star.

"Your place is in the sky with the rest of the stars. We need you to help us light up the night."

But Little Star did not want to return home.

Helen knew the red star was right, so she came up with a plan. "Come here, Little Star," she said. "I have a secret to tell you."

Little Star eagerly followed her around the corner of the house. As Helen whispered her secret, Little Star began to shine brighter and brighter. "Well, if that is true, Princess, then I must return to the sky," he said.

So Little Star and the wise red star drifted back up to the sky. "Goodbye, Helen," called Little Star.

"Goodbye, Little Star," called Helen.

As Helen climbed back into bed, Little Star looked down from above, sparkling like a diamond. The red star floated next to him.

"What did Princess Helen say to make you change your mind?" asked the red star.

"She has a special job for me," said Little Star. "I'm supposed to watch over her village and light up the sky for the frogs, crickets, goats, pigs, and all the other creatures in her kingdom. And I'm supposed to keep Princess Helen safe."

"That's a big job," said the red star. "You'll have to stay up here all the time."

"I know," said Little Star, proudly, "but this is where stars belong, isn't it?"

So on clear summer nights, when frogs croak and crickets chirp, bedtime stories echo in the air. As little girls fall asleep, the stars high above listen to these stories and watch over their dreams.

And Little Star, shining especially bright, watches over Helen and her kingdom because he knows that dreams really can come true.

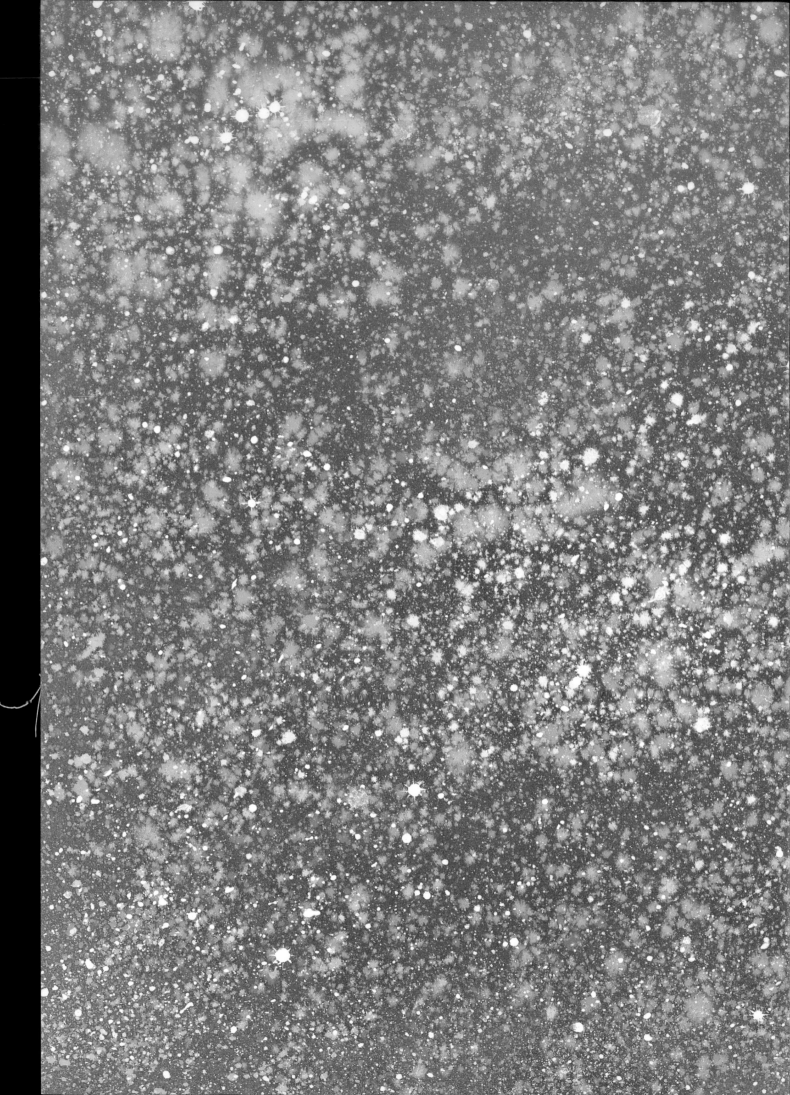